ABDO Publishing Company is the exclusive school and library distributor of Rabbit Ears Books.

Library bound edition 2005.

Library of Congress Cataloging-in-Publication Data

Roberts, Tom, 1944-
  The three little pigs / adapted by Tom Roberts ; illustrated by David Jorgensen.
     p. cm.
  "Rabbit Ears books."
  Summary: The adventures of three little pigs who leave home to seek their fortunes and how they deal with the big bad wolf.
  ISBN 1-59197-775-X
  [1. Pigs—Folklore. 2. Wolves—Folklore. 3. Folklore.] I. Jorgensen, David, ill. II. Three little pigs. English. III. Title.

PZ8.1.R527Th 2004
398.24'529734—dc22
[E]

2004047321

All Rabbit Ears books are reinforced library binding
and manufactured in the United States of America.

ABDO
Publishing Company

adapted by Tom Roberts

The Three Little Pigs

illustrated by David Jorgensen

Rabbit Ears Books

Too poor to feed them, an old mother pig sent her three little pigs off to make their own way in the world. Now let me tell you, these little pigs were as different from each other as molasses is from turpentine.

The first little pig met a man hauling a heap of straw on his back.

"Oh good sir," piped the pig, "may I please have that heap of straw?"

Well, the day was hotter than a firecracker, so the man gladly parted with his burden. And the little pig built herself a fine flaxen house.

Before long, a big old wolf wandered by, saw the little pig and knocked on the door.

"Yo, howya doing today, little pig," smiled the wolf, his empty stomach growling. "I'm hankering for a cup of coffee, won't you let me in?"

"No no no no no no, Mr. Wolf," quivered the pig, "I will not let you in. I swear by the hair on my chinny chin chin."

The wolf sneered back, "Well then, I'll huff and I'll puff and I'll blow your house in."

And he did just that. He blew down the house, grabbed the first little pig and ate her all up.

The second little pig, meanwhile, met a man lugging a load of sticks. "Oh sir," pleaded the pig, "may I please have that load of sticks?"

Well, it was getting dark, so the man willingly set down the sticks. And the second little pig built herself a wonderful wooden house.

Wouldn't you know, that same old wolf strolled by, saw the little pig, and knocked on the door.

"Yo! howya doing today little pig," grinned the wolf, his long teeth gleaming. "Whatcha been doing with youself – you're looking so fine. Won't you let me in?"

"No no, Mr. Wolf," shrieked the pig, "I will not let you in. I swear by the hair on my chinny chin chin."

The wolf leered back, "Why, I'm gonna huff and I'm gonna puff and I'll blow your house in."

So he huffed. The stick house shivered. And he puffed. The stick house shook. Then he puffed again. And the little stick house blew clean into the middle of next week. The wolf grabbed the second little pig and ate her all up.

Well, the third little pig had met the man with the heap of straw and the man with the load of sticks, but she had passed them both by. Finally, the third little pig met a man carrying a cargo of bricks.

"Oh, how are you today sir," said the pig, "May I please have that cargo of bricks?"

Well, the man was very weary, for the bricks were as heavy as a bucket of lead. So he set them down and the third little pig built herself a strong, sturdy house.

By now, sensing a trend, the wolf was on the prowl for little pigs in flimsy houses. Pretty soon he spied the third little pig and knocked on the door.

"Yo, pig," barked the wolf, not wasting time on pleasantries. "Let me in."

"No, Mr. Wolf," declared the pig, "I will not let you in. I swear by the hair on my chinny chin chin."

The wolf jeered back, "Why then, I'll huff and I'll puff and I'll blow your house in."

So he huffed. And he puffed. Then he huffed again. The little brick house didn't budge. He puffed again and huffed again. He huffed and puffed and huffed so hard he lost his breath and felt all dizzy. And still the little house held firm.

The wolf was not pleased. But wolves are clever creatures. He thought of another approach.

Tap tap tap went the wolf on the window of the little brick house.
"Hey, little pig," he coaxed. "Farmer Foster's field is just jam packed with turnips. I'll meet you here at six tomorrow morning and we can chow down together."

The little pig smiled, safe in her sturdy brick house. She knew the wolf was planning to make a meal of her. So the little pig got up at five the next morning and went alone to Farmer Foster's field. When the wolf arrived at the little brick house at six, the pig was back inside munching on a tasty turnip breakfast.

"Little pig," cooed the wolf, "are you all set?"

"Oh, out of bed, already fed, and all set for my nap," replied the pig, swallowing the last turnip.

The wolf wasn't pleased. But wolves are clever creatures. He thought of another approach.

"Oh ya cool little pig – that's cool," said the wolf, "but there are ripe, juicy apples fairly falling from the trees over at the Fortunate Orchard. I'll meet you here at five tomorrow morning and we can go have some breakfast together."

The little pig smiled.

She got up at four the next morning and went alone to the Fortunate Orchard. She was high up in a tree picking apples when the wolf arrived.

"How's the fruit?" asked the wolf, seeing the pig way up out of his reach.

"Oh, ripe and red and better than you said," announced the pig, gnawing at an especially appealing apple. "Why don't you try one for yourself, Mr. Wolf?"

With that, the pig hurled an apple as far as she could, to the far side of the orchard. Now, besides being clever, wolves are creatures of instinct. So when he saw the apple soaring across the orchard, the wolf, just like a yard dog, bounded off to fetch it. With the wolf at the edge of the orchard, the little pig slid down the tree and scurried home as fast as a grasshopper on a griddle.

The wolf returned to the tree and he realized he'd been tricked again. He was not pleased. But wolves are clever creatures. He thought of another approach.

"Howya doin', little pig?" cajoled the wolf later on, tapping at the window of the little brick house. "Today is the day of the Shanklin fair. I shall be back at three and we can go there together."

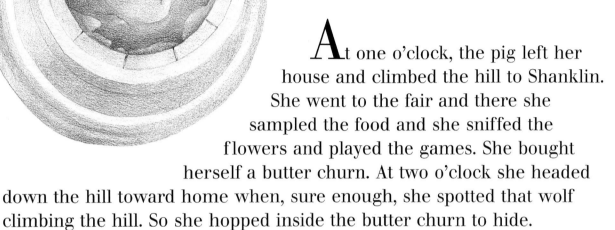

At one o'clock, the pig left her house and climbed the hill to Shanklin. She went to the fair and there she sampled the food and she sniffed the flowers and played the games. She bought herself a butter churn. At two o'clock she headed down the hill toward home when, sure enough, she spotted that wolf climbing the hill. So she hopped inside the butter churn to hide.

The churn tipped over and started to roll. Faster and faster it tumbled down the hill, 'til it was spinning like a pinwheel.

The wolf meanwhile was trudging up the hill, when all at once he heard a frightening sound. He looked up and saw, for just an instant, a blur of whirring wood. Then the churn with the pig inside rolled over the wolf like a steamroller over a cream puff. The wolf picked himself up, ran all the way home, and he never made it to the fair.

That evening, the pig sat snug as a bug in a rug in her little brick house and boiled up a great kettle of water to stew some meat for supper. Soon, a tap came on the window. It was that wolf.

"Hi. Where were you today?" asked the pig.

"A great wooden monster came roaring down the hill from Shanklin and trampled me under his hooves," explained the wolf, still picking splinters from his backside.

"Oh. Wooden, you say, Mr. Wolf?" wondered the pig.

"Wooden, yes, and as big as a barn," marveled the wolf.

The pig laughed. "It was I who frightened you. The barn that battered you was only the butter churn I bought at the fair."

The wolf felt humiliated and turned suddenly furious. "This is too much, you little ham hock!" he bellowed, and he leapt up onto the roof of the little brick house. "I am coming down the chimney and I'm going to bite you so hard it will hurt your parents and then I'm going to eat you all up."

Whistling calmly, the little pig walked across the room to the fireplace and lifted the lid off the boiling kettle of water. Just then, the wolf came roaring down the chimney and landed smack in the middle of the boiling water.

Well, the wolf got boiled into a fine stew that lasted the little pig for many delicious meals.

Yes, wolves are clever creatures, but pigs are even cleverer.